AF448047

Black Rose of the Aude Title

Lenne Arets

Copyright © 2020 Lenne Arets

All rights reserved.

ISBN:

DEDICATION

To my family.

CONTENTS

ACKNOWLEDGMENTS

I want to thank my family for their support. But especially for the encouragement to write.

1. A NEW PRIEST

"Forgive me father, for I have sinned."

That's how it always start, and it will remain so. The flesh is weak, as is the spirit. Jean-Claude was weak, just like his mind. He sold his soul for fifty gold francs an let without son. He had enough money to continue his life somewhere unnoticed. To save my honour, Gabriel had even staged a funeral mass. The whole village had come out to mourn the accidental husband and son, and to comfort the young widow. Gabriel had offered me the position of housekeeper. As a good Christian, he would take care of every resident of his parish. Likewise, for the grieving widow. Despite the loss of Jean-Claude, I fell in love with the new priest. There was something magical about him, something elusive, and I wanted to find out that.

Gabriel, who appeard out of nowhere as a new priest in our village two years ago, surrounded by mysteries, moved into the old, dilapidated rectory atop the hill. Curious villagers would sit in church every Sunday. Curious about what the new priest had to say. After the previous priest's death, we had been without a clergyman for at least a year, once the bishop came with his entourage. After being received by the mayor and richly supplied with food and drink, he returned to the bishop's palace in Carcassonne. After that, it was quiet until the young priest appeared in the village suddenly. Gabriel, even his name sounded heavenly.

I crawled behind the confessional through a door in het hallway. Gabriel pionted me to this secret place without saying anything. His dark, piercing eyes seemed to say, "Take advantage of it."

Whenever someone comes to confess in the rectory, I quietly take a seat behind the thin wooden wall.

"Forgive me father, because I have sinned."

Similarly, I heard a strange female voice that day. I was sure she's not from the village, because I knew everyone and their pathetic secrets. I was right behind Gabriel. Stroke the wood with my fingertips. I could almost touch him. The thought of being separated from him by a few planks excited me enormously. I slowly rubbed my hand over my long skirt, pulled it up, and rubbed between my legs.

"What do you want to say?" I heard him ask. His voice was like honey.

Sweet, warm and sticky. I sighed, hoping the woman, on the other end, didn't hear.

"I'm talking to my dead husband,"she said hesitantly. "I know God had forbidden talking to the dead, but I miss him so much." She almost sobbed. Then, that sweet voice again. I prick up my ears.

"There is a possibility," Gabriel said almost in a whisper, "but you must keep it a secret."

"Of course, father. I'll do whatever you say." The woman sounded hopeful.

"Come back on Sunday evening after sunset. Make sure no one sees you and don't talk to anyone about it. My housekeeper will give you further instructions." Gabriel said.

I quickly withdrew my hand from my crotch an smoothed my skirt. Silently I left the secret room and waited for the woman in the vestibule. The door to the large drawing-room opened, and she carefully stepped into the long narrow corridor. Her face was hidden under a large black wide-brimmed hat with a cascade of tulle. As it would be for a good widow, she was dressed all in black like me, with the difference that her dress is made of silk. My simple waitress dress was made of cotton, with a cream-coloured apron.

"Come after sunset on Sunday evening, let your driver wait behind the rectory by the trees and make sure you don't get seen," I said to her coolly. "And you should bring a hundred francs, don't forget that."

"A hundred francs?" She asked in astonishment, "That's a whole month's salary."

In silence, I held the door open for her. She stepped outside, shaking her head. Since Gabriel had left the confessional, he was standing close to me in the hallway. I smelled his heavenly body scent and immediately felt weak again when I looked into those dark eyes. I seem to be sucked into the universe.

"Is she coming on Sunday?" Gabriel asked in a whisper in my ear.

"I don't know. She had some reservations about the money," I replied softly.

He put his arms around my waist and kissed me on my right cheek. "Maybe you should try harder; we both know what we're doing it for," he said softly. But the words hit me like a hammer blow. The undertone had something compelling about it. Of course, I knew what I was doing it for.

"I'd like to build a personal library," his words sounded almost childish. "We both have to work hard for that."
His hands had found their way to my breasts, gentle caresses that slowly turned to squeeze. "We'll finish this tonight," he said as he headed toward the kitchen. I checked the clock in the hall; half-past twelve, time for lunch.

2. MISTRAL

To buy off their salvation, the villagers and farmers in the area provided us with plenty of food and drink. Gabriel had made it very clear during his first mass here, that he was a priest without stipends and this was the only way for our village to get closer to God. Other priests wouldn't give up their parishes, and the bishop had seen only one more opportunity: Gabriel.

He would wipe out evil. The villagers had looked at each other in surprise, thinking of what evil? But the fire which Gabriel defended his sermon raised no further questions. Despite the poverty in the village, the people gave what they could spare. Convinced that they could buy themselves into the afterlife, they lavishly filled the collection basket after the mass. Gabriel had asked Jean-Claude after mass that why he had not put a franc in the basket. To which my husband replied that he did not believe in that nonsense. Not shortly afterwards, both Jean-Claude and our son had disappeared.

Gabriel was very open and direct about it to me. He showed a receipt of fifty gold francs. At the bottom of the note, there was the name of Jean-Claude in shaky handwriting. I had looked at Gabriel in disbelief when he came to see me. I burst into rage and scratched his left cheeck. That same evening he laid in my marital bed, where we first passionately made love and divised a plan to deal with this situation. Even before the rooster crows, he left for the presbytery.

I poured him a large glass of wine and cut the bread into thick slices. I took a cup of milk for myself because I was not very hungry. The summer heat had taken over the presbytery. I felt tired and nauseous. The sounds of the construction workers in the background thundered through the walls and caused an severe headache.

"This afternoon, I'm at church, preparing to unveil the new baptismal font," Gabriel said.

"I'm curious what the villagers think of that," I answered. "It's daring, to say the least."

"The villagers have to see where their money is being spent," he said, stroking my cheeck.

"Then again, I haven't been to a church where a statue of the devil holds the baptismal font," I said.

"But this village has an execptional church," Gabriel winked at me.

"I'm going to get the big drawing-room ready for Sunday," I said, placing the empty cup on a low wooden cupboard. "Unless you still need to take special confessions."

"No, I no longer have any special agreements; you can already preprare everything."

I walked outsitde, hoping to cool off. But the warm Mistral wind from the Pyrenees played an unbeatable game. For millions of years, this wind had a grip on the landscape. Mountain ranges have been reduced to rolling hills. From the corner of my eye, I saw five construction workers busy with large, light yellow rectangular blocks of sandstone. After het rectory was completely renovated, the builders started on the next project; a large square tower complete with medieval battements and pointed arch windows. They were only halfway through construction, but the sandstone building had already dominated the landscape. I wondered how long this building would hold his shape before the Mistral regains its grip on it. A few weeks ago, the mayor had complained about the monstrous building under construction. Gabriel had welcomed him in the great drawing-room. I had to provide them with a carafe of good wine. An hour later and an empty carafe as a silent witness, the mayor staggered down the narrow path towards the village.

"We Won't be bothered by that for now," Gabriel had said confidently. I don't know what Gabriel discussed with the mayor, but I thought it was magical. No one could win over the mayor like Gabriel. Not even the notary, who had a lot of power in the village. Since then, the front bench in the church had been reserved for the mayor and his family. The notary had to settle for the second bench. Behind the second bench sat the well-tot-do bourgeoisie, the villagers and farmers from the area had to settle for the chruch's rear part. Often they still had to stand, as the church was too small to seat them all. In fact, the church was a proper chapel, where a piece added. Gabriel had decided that not only had to be invested heavily in the renovation of the rectory, but also for the church. I should become the most controversial church in the Aude.

I heard the men talking behind my back, heard my name fall, and a lot of laughter.

"What's there to laugh about? Shouldn't you keep on working?" I asked, slightly irritated.

"Look, the devil's whore is trying to put us to work," said one of the men.

Angry, I walked up to him. "Whore of the devil?" I asked the person who came first. He quickly turned his head and pulled his cap over his eyes.

"What shall I do? Give you the evil eye of tell the priest?" I asked angrily.

"Please not," he begged form under his cap, quickly signing the cross.

Anger overtook me, I wanted to scream, push him over the edge and into the abyss, but I controlled myself and walked back to the kitchen. I angrily smashed the cup on the ground. How dare he called me a whore? My husband sold me for fifty fucking gold francs. The Judas. The noise had caught Gabriel's attention.

"Everything alright?" he asked looking into the kitchen in the doorway.

"Yes," I said, leaning against the table, "I bumped into the cup." I didn't dare look at him, afraid that he sees my anger; I didn't feel like explaining it. Maybe he would have fired the workers, and that tower was so important for him.

"I'm fine, go to church," I said. With my head bowed, I walked behind him in the hallway and watched him walk through the backyard towards the church that was two hundred meters behind the garden. Separated from tall trees an thickets, only the spire of the small house of worship was visible.

3. DRAWING-ROOM

To buy off their salvation, the villagers and farmers in the area provided us with plenty of food and drink. Gabriel had made it very clear during his first mass here, that he was a priest without stipends and this was the only way for our village to get closer to God. Other priests wouldn't give up their parishes, and the bishop had seen only one more opportunity: Gabriel.

He would wipe out evil. The villagers had looked at each other in surprise, thinking of what evil? But the fire which Gabriel defended his sermon raised no further questions. Despite the poverty in the village, the people gave what they could spare. Convinced that they could buy themselves into the afterlife, they lavishly filled the collection basket after the mass. Gabriel had asked Jean-Claude after mass that why he had not put a franc in the basket. To which my husband replied that he did not believe in that nonsense. Not shortly afterwards, both Jean-Claude and our son had disappeared.

Gabriel was very open and direct about it to me. He showed a receipt of fifty gold francs. At the bottom of the note, there was the name of Jean-Claude in shaky handwriting. I had looked at Gabriel in disbelief when he came to see me. I burst into rage and scratched his left cheeck. That same evening he laid in my marital bed, where we first passionately made love and divised a plan to deal with this situation. Even before the rooster crows, he left for the presbytery.

I poured him a large glass of wine and cut the bread into thick slices. I took a cup of milk for myself because I was not very hungry. The summer heat had taken over the presbytery. I felt tired and nauseous. The sounds of the construction workers in the background thundered through the walls and caused an severe headache.

"This afternoon, I'm at church, preparing to unveil the new baptismal font," Gabriel said.

"I'm curious what the villagers think of that," I answered. "It's daring, to say the least."

"The villagers have to see where their money is being spent," he said, stroking my cheeck.

"Then again, I haven't been to a church where a statue of the devil holds the baptismal font," I said.

"But this village has an execptional church," Gabriel winked at me.

"I'm going to get the big drawing-room ready for Sunday," I said, placing the empty cup on a low wooden cupboard. "Unless you still need to take special confessions."

"No, I no longer have any special agreements; you can already preprare everything."

I walked outsitde, hoping to cool off. But the warm Mistral wind from the Pyrenees played an unbeatable game. For millions of years, this wind had a grip on the landscape. Mountain ranges have been reduced to rolling hills. From the corner of my eye, I saw five construction workers busy with large, light yellow rectangular blocks of sandstone. After het rectory was completely renovated, the builders started on the next project; a large square tower complete with medieval battements and pointed arch windows. They were only halfway through construction, but the sandstone building had already dominated the landscape. I wondered how long this building would hold his shape before the Mistral regains its grip on it. A few weeks ago, the mayor had complained about the monstrous building under construction. Gabriel had welcomed him in the great drawing-room. I had to provide them with a carafe of good wine. An hour later and an empty carafe as a silent witness, the mayor staggered down the narrow path towards the village.

"We Won't be bothered by that for now," Gabriel had said confidently. I don't know what Gabriel discussed with the mayor, but I thought it was magical. No one could win over the mayor like Gabriel. Not even the notary, who had a lot of power in the village. Since then, the front bench in the church had been reserved for the mayor and his family. The notary had to settle for the second bench. Behind the second bench sat the well-tot-do bourgeoisie, the villagers and farmers from the area had to settle for the chruch's rear part. Often they still had to stand, as the church was too small to seat them all. In fact, the church was a proper chapel, where a piece added. Gabriel had decided that not only had to be invested heavily in the renovation of the rectory, but also for the church. I should become the most controversial church in the Aude.

I heard the men talking behind my back, heard my name fall, and a lot of laughter.

"What's there to laugh about? Shouldn't you keep on working?" I asked, slightly irritated.

"Look, the devil's whore is trying to put us to work," said one of the men.

Angry, I walked up to him. "Whore of the devil?" I asked the person who came first. He quickly turned his head and pulled his cap over his eyes.

"What shall I do? Give you the evil eye of tell the priest?" I asked angrily.

"Please not," he begged form under his cap, quickly signing the cross.

Anger overtook me, I wanted to scream, push him over the edge and into the abyss, but I controlled myself and walked back to the kitchen. I angrily smashed the cup on the ground. How dare he called me a whore? My husband sold me for fifty fucking gold francs. The Judas. The noise had caught Gabriel's attention.

"Everything alright?" he asked looking into the kitchen in the doorway.

"Yes," I said, leaning against the table, "I bumped into the cup." I didn't dare look at him, afraid that he sees my anger; I didn't feel like explaining it. Maybe he would have fired the workers, and that tower was so important for him.

"I'm fine, go to church," I said. With my head bowed, I walked behind him in the hallway and watched him walk through the backyard towards the church that was two hundred meters behind the garden. Separated from tall trees an thickets, only the spire of the small house of worship was visible.

4. SORRY

"We can do something about that." Gabriel took my hand and pulled me towards the house. He started to kiss me passionately in the hall and slowly pushed me up the stairs while kissing. At the top, I lost my balance and fell on my buttocks on the landing. Gabriel looked at me eagerly, pushed my long skirt up, and pulled down my underpants in one go. He held up his habit with one hand and climbed on top of me. No sympathy this time; he penetrated me with a lot of violence. My back hurt on the hard plank floor. I saw a hellish red fire in his eyes and turned my head to the side. I didn't want to look at him. But with his hand, he firmly grasped my jaw and turned my head back.

"I want you to look at me," he hissed. This is what you want, right? You want me to take you, don't you?" He said. I kept my eyes closed an felt him penetrate even deeper.

"It hurts," I groaned. When I opened my eyes, I saw his devilish look just above me; hypnotically, he pulled me straight into hell. My future in the hereafter was fixed. He kept going, the pain travelled through my abdominal cavity towards my lungs, and I gasped for breath. I felt light-headed an afraid that I might pass out. Fortunately, he was withdrawing. Panting, he hanged over me and I let my tears run free.

"What is it?" He asked with a groan.

"One of the handyman instulted me," I said with a pain in my stomach. I was afraid to tell him that I was terrified of him. That would have only excited him more.

Gabriel straightened up and adjusted his habit. Without saying a word, he descended the stairs again, towards the front door. Completely stunned, I sat at top of the stairs. What had just happened? Had he raped me? Usually, he didn't act like that. And then that scary look in his eyes…

I got up and went to the bathroom. It was still hurting; even walking was difficult. I poured cold water from a jug into a bowl and refreshed myself al little. The cold water burned my intimate parts, and I was doubled over in pain. "What should I do?" I thought. I couldn't go to the doctor, who would have immediately asked many questions. "What would I tell him? That I have been with a man during my mourning period? That is impossible." I thought. My personal hell would immediately begin there in the village. I would be banned. Where should I go?

Questions keep running through my head. To distract myself from hell and damnation, I decided to cook dinner. Slowly, I stumbled down to the kitchen. From the cellar, I got potatoes and vegetables. I had to do was heat up the meat while cooking the potatoes and vegetables. I heard a lot of stumbling; presumably, Gabriel had returned home. I really didn't feel like him and kept concentrating on the food. After half an hour, we could sit down for dinner. I didn't have to call him; it seemed he smelled the food. He walked into the kitchen confidently and sat at the table without saying anything. Silently I scooped the food on two plates and put them on the table. Gabriel folded his hands and began a prayer of thanks. In him imitation, I also folded my hands but kept staring at my plate.

"You forgot the wine," he said monotonously. I got up and took two cups from the shelf. From the pantry, I took a stone carafe filled with red wine. With a bang, I put the carafe on the table. Red wine splashed over the rim, and without looking at Gabriel, I put a matching stone cup in front of him. I sat down, thinking the piece of meat in the pan was Gabriel's brisket, and forcefully inserted the large meat fork into the roast. Gabriel didn't give a kick, and I expected him to pour the wine for us, as usual. But instead, he got up and reached into one of the pockets of his black habit. I kept staring at the meat fork in the roast, while I laid my right arm relaxed on the table as inconspicuously as possible. Close to the frying pan. Gabriel stood behind me and leaned forward. I held my breath; all the muscles of my body were under high tension. When he touched me, I struck.

"I'm sorry about later," he said remorsefully. Relieved, I took a breath but left my arm close to the pan just to be sure. The meat fork at my fingertips. I heard his habit rustle and suddenly felt his two hands around my neck. I gasped, he won't...

Before I knew, I had a gold necklace with a cameo pendant around my neck. Surpised, I took the pendant in my left hand an studied it carefully; a female profile carved from white stone on a red coral backgroud, set in a golden oval frame.

"But..." I stammered, getting no further.

Gabriel sat down at the table again an cut the meat as if nothing was wrong. We talked a little about trivial things and forgot about the afternoon's incident. After dinner, I cleaned up and rinsed the plates and cutlery. I was startled by the shrill doorbell. I quickly dried my hands and wanted to walk into the hall, but Gabriel was ahead of me. He was in the hall, closing the door in my face. A moment later, I heard a man talking to him, and then closing the front door. Gabriel's footsteps were headed this way. I quickly resumed the dishes and tried to behave as casually as possible. He entered the kitchen with a closed box and immediately continued towards the cellar. After a few minutes, he was back next to me.

"Did you like the necklace?"

"Yes it's beautiful," I answered, holding back my tears. He gently caressed my neck and then ran his hand over my back to my buttocks. Instinctively, I stepped forward but was stopped by the worktop with the water bowl on it. I had nowhere to go, and my heart started to beat faster again. He left the kitchen with a playful tap against my buttocks an headed for the study. I put my ear against the study door, heard him rumbling inside. I quickly took a gas lamp from the top shelf, lit it, and walked down the basement stairs with it. The small flame gave just enough light to see the immediate surroundings. Fortunately, we had electric light throughout the house, except in the basement. At the bottom of the stairs, there was the wooden box that Gabriel had just placed there. I let the lamp pass over the boarded-up box. Strange figures and signs were branded in the wood. I recognized some, such as an inverted cross and a pentagram, but couldn't recognise many. I looked like a different language, a kind of cypher. The box gave no further clues, and I walked up the stairs again. Turned off the gas lamp an put it back on the shelf. Fortunately, we had electric light throughout the house, except in the basement.

5. MYSTERIOUS TELEGRAM

Gabriel had promised that when the tower is finished, he will make sure that we would also have running water in the kitchen and a real bathroom. Around half-past nine in the evening, I decided to go to bed. I opened the maid's bedroom. I was no longer a virgin, but that night I wanted to rest and be left alone.

That night I had a restless dream; I kept seeing that strange glow in Gabriel's eyes. In the morning, when I woke up from the crowing of the cock, I couldn't say that I feel rested. I got dressed and went downstairs to prepare breakfast. The baker had already placed a basket of freshly baked bread rolls at the front door. I boiled water for coffee and got the butter, cheese and jam from the pantry. Gabriel entered the kitchen in a much better mood. He stroked my neck and asked where the necklace is.

"I left it upstairs; I don't want the workers to see it. That would only make more gossip," I told him. He nodded in agreement and walked to the kitchen window. Outside, the masons were already busy.

I heard a lot of excited voices. "Why are they making such a noise?" I asked curiously.

"The library must be ready for All Souls' Day." Gabriel was still staring out the window.

"What has All Souls' Day to do with it?" I didn't understand him.

He turned and walked over to me, took my face in both hands, and looked straight at me: "Because of the drama."

For a moment, I thought I saw the entrance gate of hell again in his eyes. "Oh," was all I could say and Gabriel let go of my face.

"I spend the rest of the day in my study and want to be able to word undisturbed," he instructed as he walked along the rack with the serving spoons.

"Where's the meat fork?" He asked as he passed and before disapearing into the basement.

"It's among the dirty dishes," I called out into the dark hole, hoping he heard this.

Moments later, he came upstairs with the branded wooden box and immediately disappeared toward the study. I saw my chance and picked up my knitted shawl for a hook in the hallway. Wrapped it around my shoulders, and I managed to reach the gravel path down through the back door. I walked fast, and after twenty minutes, I arrived in the village. I walked up the main street towards the post office. Fortunately, this was still open on Saturday morning.

The postal worker sat behind a wooden counter on which a glass wall had been placed for safety. A recess in the glass allowed customers and office workers to exchange forms and money.

"I'd like to send a telegram to Toulouse," I told him.

An older man with a colossal moustache looked at me suspiciously. I shoved a few francs through the opening.

"Great," said the man gruffly, "What should it contain and what is the delivery address?"

"When will the telegram be delivered?" I asked.

"Monday." His tone had not gotten any brighter.

"Then put in, *Tuesday*," I said firmly.

Surprised, the postal worker looked at me. "And further?" He asked.

"Nothing else," I replied.

He took the money from the counter and put it in order. "To which address should the telegram be sent an to whom should the name be sent?" he asked.

" Just let the telegram arrive at the post office, without a name." I was starting to feel a little uncomfortable.

"That's very unusual, lady," he said sternly. I could see the contempt in his look. The priest's housekeeper was up to something. You just saw him thinking it. He started drafting the telegram and finally noted the address of the post office in Toulouse.

"Can I be sure the telegram will be at the post office Monday?" I asked, just to be sure.

"Madame, the French Postal Services won't let you down. We work extremely accurately," he said with a haughty look in his eyes. I nodded politely at him and got out of there as soon as possible. Outside, I sniffed the warm wind. It promised to be another hot day. I was almost starting to feel sorry for the construction workers. Especially when Gabriel had increased the workload. I decided to go back to the rectory on the hill. The way back once took so long. The heat was starting to hit, and I was struggling to make progress. When I arrived at the top, I walked behind the church to the water pump. When I passed the church, I thought I heard groans. I stopped for a moment to listen. No, this must be the wind. At the water pump, I put my heated head entirely under the ice water jet for a few minutes and walked into the kitchen with soaking wet and dripping hair. Gabriel was nowhere to be seen. Probably he was still in the study. I put a kettle of water on the woodstove.

6. ILLUSTRIOUS COMPANY

"Where were you?" Gabriel was suddenly behind me. "Did you fall into the water?" He asked, running his hand through my wet hair.

"I was hot," I said, my heart was pounding in my throat. His jet-black eyes pierced my skull, and I felt a sharp headache coming on.

"Don't lie to me," I heard him say before passing out. I didn't know how long I'd been out, but when I woke up I was lying on the bed in the master bedroom full fully clothed. Outside it was already getting gloaming. It looked like it won't be long before it was completely dark. I slowly sit up; my dress was crumpled. I rubbed the folds roughly to get it somewhat smooth. The headache was still dominant, and I staggered to the door like a drunkard. I stopped on the landing, some voices came from the study. Gabriel had a visitor. I didn't feel like facing him, turned around, and walked back into the bedroom. I undress, put my dress and apron over the chair by the bed. I took my nightdress from under the pillow and put it over my head before getting into bed. I soon fell into a deep, dreamless sleep.

In the distance, I heard a rooster crowing and felt trapped by a heavy man's arm. Gabriel was lying in bed next to me, holding me tight. I could hear his calm, rhythmic breathing that he was still asleep. I carefully tried to wriggle free. A sigh escaped from his mouth. As I took my clothes off the chair, my gaze fell on the brown leather suitcase on top of the wardrobe. The suitcase with which Gabriel entered the village, his only possession. I got dressed and sneaked out of the bedroom My adoration for him had given way to pure fear.

In the kitchen, I made sure that breakfast was ready. Gabriel could come down at any time. Today was going to be a busy day; an early morning mass and another Sunday mass at three this afternoon. And then, of course, tonight...

The most important thing of the day, what do I say, of the whole week, Gabriel lived for that night's activities. Financial returns aside, he took great pleasure in deceiving people. But on the other hand, I got the impression that the people participating in those sessions were only too happy to pay for that nonsense. Because that was it, pure nonsense topped with a sauce of occultism, magic and demonology.

He stood fresh and delighted in the doorway. Smiling broadly, he sat down at the breakfast table and let the soft-boiled egg taste good. Thus he resembled the man I felt for; an angel. After freshening up, he kissed my cheeks and left for church. Soon after, I heard the bells rang as a sign that the villagers must have left for the hill to save their souls. I washed the dishes and went back to the bedroom to make the bed. My gaze fell back to his suitcase. I slid the chair against the wardrobe ad climbed it so that I could take the suitcase off the wardrobe. Although the weight suggested something in it, I was disappointed when the suitcase turned empty. I gently rubbed the inner lining with my left hand. Interestingly, I felt something. I Carefully inspected the silky soft fabric, an saw that a seam with coarse stitches had been secured again.

I looked across the room; there was my sewing box on a small table. I put the suitcase opened on the bed and got a pair of scissors from the sewing box. I carefully cut the stitches without damaging the thin fabric. I reached into the opening with my hand and felt the paper. Between my thumb and forefinger, I took several papers. To my great surprise, those papers turned out to be banknotes; all one hundred franc notes. I quickly counted the notes in my hand. Twenty-five and in the secret compartment of the trunk, there were even more. I put the banknotes back en searched th sewing box for a needle and thread. I carefully sewed the opening closed with coarse stitches. I closed the suitcase and put it back in the same position on the wardrobe.

Gabriel came home alone for lunch and immediately left for church. I kept walking around the house, restlessly for the rest of the afternoon. I couldn't concentrate and decided to make preparations for the night. I got four bottles of red wine from the cellar, which I immediately took to the large drawing-room. There I put them on one of the smaller tables along the wall. I got six crystal glasses from a display cabinet. Just like the wooden box that was recently delivered, those wine glasses bore the same mysterious markings. I put the glasses on the large table and uncorked two of the four bottles. I slowly poured the dark red liquid into two decanters and placed them on the table with the glasses. I left the other two bottles on the side table. Then I turned on the chandelier and closed the heavy curtains. Every trace of light was kept out. When I left the drawing-room, I turned the light off and closed the door, leaving the haunting darkness behind me.

In the hallway, I stopped in front of the door to the study. I could only enter it when Gabriel was there. I instinctively looked around as I pushed the door handle down and then stepped into the room. The wooden box with the mysterious characters was open on the desk. I glanced back to make sure Gabriel wasn't around before glancing inside the chest.

A special object lay on black velvet, a golden bar with a golden pear on it. I carefully took the object out of the box. It was still quite heavy, and I wondered if it was gold. The pear didn't appear massive and had longitudinal seams. "What would Gabriel do with this?" I asked myself. I put it back in the box, left the room, and closed the door behind me.

Later that afternoon, Gabriel returned and immediately locked himself in the study. I knocked on the door and asked if he would like something to eat. "Not hungry," he replied.

He finally came out of the study at around seven o'clock. He carried the chest in his hands, which he immediately took to the large drawing-room. He spent the time until sunset in the corridor, walking restlessly back and forth. The doorbell rang, and I answered. The mayor was on the doorstep, and I gave him a warm welcome. Then I took his coat, and Gabriel took him to the drawing-room. Then the doorbell rang again, this time the notary. He, too, was received with all respect and led to the lounge. So it went on three more times, the unknown woman in black also reappeared. When all the guests were in the grand drawing-room, I locked the front door and joined the illustrious company. The salon was lit exclusively by candles in five-armed crystal candlesticks. The group was around the table with a glass of wine in their hand. Gabriel monotonously muttered unknown prayers, and the lady and gentlemen repeated them in the same tone. Then they took a seat behind the table and Gabriel took out an ouija plate. They held hands and evoke the ghost of the dead husband of the woman in black. In the back of the room, I waved my skirt vigorously. The airflow made the candle flames dance, and everyone was convinced that the conjured spirit was present among us.

7. TOULOUSE

Gabriel slowly let the board slide over the plate; at the behest of the ghost, the guests had to perform a task: silencing an unbeliever. The mayor and notary got up and left the room. Meanwhile, Gabriel pulled a red, shiny cape over his priestly robes. After a few minutes, the notables returned with a man chained in their midst. I recognized this one as the construction worker who called me the whore of the Devil. He was dressed only in his underpants, and his back clearly showed signs of abuse, red welts with black, dried blood as silent witnesses to lashes. Terror was in his eyes as he was put in front of the curtains. The two honorable men were still holding him tight. He had nowhere to go.
Gabriel was standing with the golden object in his hands and slowly walked towards the construction worker. Its long cloak made it appear as if it was floating. The other guests were watching breathlessly.
Then Gabriel ordered the man to open his mouth.
Gabriel put the golden pear in the man's mouth and turned the rod. The pear opened like the leaves of a flower. The man groaned and squirmed, but Gabriel spun it, and the poor man's oral cavity was stretched to the limit. A nauseating crack indicated that the unfortunate person's jaw had been shattered. He could never speak again. Gabriel now turned the bar in the opposite direction, and the golden flower closed again.
"We do this with blasphemists," he said triumphantly, holding up the seepage pear. The guests applauded. My stomach turned, and I tried not to vomit. After Gabriel talked about ghosts, those present brought out their purses. They paid with one hundred franc notes. I felt bad when I let the guests out through the back door. Lousy about what I'd seen, lousy about what Gabriel was capable of.
As I walked past the study, I saw Gabriel dragging the man out. I kept watching them from a safe distance, but couldn't see anything through the darkness. Then I heard an icy scream that disappeared into the distance.
Oh, God, he pushed him into the abyss. In a panic, I ran upstairs to the bedroom, locked the door, and put another chair against the door. If he

would try to come in, at least I would hear it. I walked restlessly through space. "Where should I go? I have nowhere to go," I thought. Tired, I fell onto the bed and cried myself to sleep.

It was still dark. There was something in the bedroom; I could feel it. The chair was still against the door, but I perceived a presence with all my senses. Suddenly, I was pushed back into the pillows. A hand over my mouth prevented me from screaming. I recognized the Devil's look. Gabriel!

How did he get in? Blind panic overtook me, but he was stronger. He sat on top of me and grinned demonically. He slowly bent over and tried to kiss me. I quickly grabbed the meat fork from under the mattress and pushed the two sharp ends into his neck with all my strength. Blood spurted from the two big holes, and a pitiful screech came from his mouth. I pushed even harder into the flesh with all my might. The last thing I saw in his eyes was unbelief.

Cold moonlight shined over his dead, pale face. The meat fork was still in his neck. My heart was pounding when I saw plumes of smoke rising from the two holes. A burning smell, I smelled a burning smell. His depraved body seemed to catch fire. Horrified, I jumped out of bed, threw the chair aside, and turned the key. I ran down the stairs to the patio. I didn't know what to do. Death surrounded me, upstairs in the bedroom and down in the ravine. I was freezing, despite the balmy night and I didn't want to go back into the house. I spent the rest of the night in his library under construction.

The next morning I woke up stiff, stretch, and slowly walked back to the house. In the kitchen, I considered going to the bedroom. What if I had this dream? And Gabriel was just in bed? Armed with the largest carving knife, I crept up the stairs. The bedroom door was still ajar, and a burning smell was coming towards me. The bed was like a battlefield, drenched in blood and the meat fork was in the middle of a mountain of ash. Nobody to be seen, totally burned. Bewildered, I looked at the scene and wondered how this is possible. I quickly climbed onto the chair and took the suitcase from the cupboard. I threw in some items of clothing and walked to the door.

"You had a different goal than I did, Gabriel," I said before I left. Outside the village, I got a lift on a farm cart. I was in Toulouse the next day, with Jean-Claude and my son.

ABOUT THE AUTHOR

Lenne Arets lives with her family and two dogs in the south of the Netherlands. She is fascinated with human behavior and how it is influenced by circumstances. She also has a great interest in history. Human behavior and history are therefore important sources of inspiration for her stories.

www.ingramcontent.com/pod-product-compliance
Lightning Source LLC
Chambersburg PA
CBHW071248140726
47996CB00007B/2799